*Banal Incidents*

*from*

*My First Period*

*by*

*JOHN RETY*

for Leah Fritz,
a bit of my life,
not all of it true
John Rety

BOX TWO/HEARING EYE

London 1993

*Also by John Rety:*

*Supersozzled Nights (Rubicon Press, 1953)*

*Song of Anarchy (Hearing Eye, 1989)*

*Paracelsus (play, unpublished, 1991)*

*Box Two/Hearing Eye*
*99 Torriano Avenue*
*London. NW5 2RX*

*ISBN 1 870841 28/X*

# I

There was nothing to it, He was going to make a living from his writing.

He was leaving home. His father fat, balding. His mother was lithe, bit perfumy, terribly pompous, little bit acting stupid, sometimes very beautiful, most of the times entertaining. What a long description and not at all complete.

What I want to concentrate on, however, is that this is a piece of writing which must pass the approbation of all who still live within me, that luggage which I carry around in my head, only use to me until I write it down in such a manner that others who may find time in their busy life to glance at it, may read it one day; poor fellow, what a curious burden you carry around, let me give you for it the price of a book; I'll try to read it on a sunny day, after I've read all the others. A shoe that is too tight sometimes has to be worn. Grimace and smile for only another dozen or so spaces, steps, alright chapters, pages to go!

II

A pink over a white damask
tablecloth. I must leave
their description to your
imagination; covers spotlessly
clean, just so, with the
diamond shaped pink cloth over
the finest white linen, the
chequered table anonymously
concealed below is where your
very own Bloom sits, in front
of him a plate of deliciously
cooked croute aux champignons,
with a brown sauce with a taste
of kidney, without which no
Arts Council grant-fed writer

may put in an expense-sheet and hope to be accepted.

This is Sabbath night and Bloom, although well in his sixth decade, has just seen two thousand years unfold and has never batted an eyelid. How do you bat an eyelid, was in Brewer's, the rest may be assured but he was not fussy as to what was meant by this peculiar expression.

Other authors more practised than he have tackled this thorny problem afore, and Bloom was not at all bothered by yet another ready-made phrase; lemon tea, golden bronze in a fluted glass in filligree silver holder on an honest brown rimmed saucer, a couple of lovers as the lights dim, as a biblical voice sings on the sound machine.

A sip takes Bloom back to childhood, that lovable without fuss tea, a sprinkle of leaves in boiling water, a slice of lemon and sugar, even rum would not spoil the taste or obscure the mood.

Only an hour ago a woman allowed him to see for the first time, so it seemed to him the first time, his memory was blank about this aspect of laying the table on the Sabbath night.

What a performance, what horrible significance. To have been shown a well laid table, but not laid for Bloom. The candlestick was unlit as he left the woman's house.

Very polite, very English, terribly funny if it were not so sad.

[Instruction to printer: here insert twenty pages from any other book at random to bulk up pages and add content.]

## III

Two poems, three accidents
and four cups of coffee later,
his pen was racing on. What a
responsibility, the music now
crackling ecclesiastical, post
coitus interruptus, the
cigarette limp in graceful
fingers as the soft hatted
woman looks bemused at the
assured young man.

The woman's voice in his
head; the hurrying steps on
the steps, other writers could
have expressed this more
elegantly, Bloom was past
caring about such niceties.

Two women offering him advice. You be a poet, you are a poet, said one. You be a hairdresser, advised the other. Fifty years later to hear this from two charmers which fifty years asince was his father's parting advice to him.

## I V

Bloom could not remember whether Bloom senior was as tall as he was now. For now he was Bloom senior's age then, but what he remembered was a younger Bloom looking at this specimen of portly humanity who went by the name of his father.

Be a poet the personage solemnly said. Wearing benignly his fatherly hat over a round Leninny balding head. Or a hairdresser. You'll always find a job in either profession. Now the mad background orchestra was struggling with the Radetzky March. In either case you'll travel the world, he said.

As a poet, I said bewildered. Did I say poet, I meant to say priest.

Priest, I exclaimed, but I don't believe in God.

And secretly Bloom thought that women would be forbidden to him. And why should he become a hairdresser, a boy lathering men's cheeks, a man messing about with other people's hair.

The interview was over, the passport stamped, the suitcase packed, farewells made and a last talk with Mother.

Paris was not possible, Tel Aviv ditto, London it had to be.

V

Who did he leave behind? Those who were dead he only left symbolically. There was no point in worshipping a shrine where somebody had performed life's necessary acts. The man dies, the woman washes the socks, underpants and into the sink the last bit of the dirt that remains of the man disappears down the plughole.

Much later a recording, the voice of the man on the answerphone 'leave a message after the blip', but that is all that is left of him. He is dead. There is no point in leaving a message. 'I'm sorry, I have just heard that you have passed into another world. I would have liked to have had your company for supper this evening, but if you're dead there is no point in my inviting you. I will just have to eat two plates of macaroni, but I don't have to open two bottles of Chianti.'

*There were people who were alive and those were the ones he left. He left them where they were. He didn't take them with him. How could he have put all his acquaintances into one suitcase and carry them across Europe on the Alberg Express. How could any brain put up with such cargo. One ticket transports one person only, but the suitcase is packed full of ancestors, kins, friends and ex-countrymen. "Carry your bag, sir?" "By all means, as long as you can lift it." "But it is as light as a feather."*

"For you it may be, for you don't know, can't feel what's inside."

There was a girl on the bed, very attractive, terribly in love, soft as a whisper and so exciting that even sixty years have not erased her from Bloom's memory. Why did he leave her behind, they were made for each other, they were in love. He could not remember the moment of their parting. "Shall I see you tomorrow as usual?" "Not unless you come and see me in London." She laughed and thought it was just one of his jokes.

# VI

Bloom's mother took him to her favourite coffee house by the Theatre. He vividly remembered the narrow long room with mirrors on both walls, fittings of chromium, a middle passage, tiny chairs and tables by the mirrors. The place was full. Everybody looked at him with interest. The boy was going to London. How lucky you are. A very ugly man disagreed. "You are making the biggest mistake of your life. You'll remember my words all your life. There is no world outside these walls. You'll rue the day you leave." Young Bloom was annoyed by the jarring voice, he preferred to be deemed lucky.

By that time Grandmother was dead. She died nearly three years previous. He would never leave her behind although she was torn from him.

Unbelievable unluck her killing, as it was described to him, this awful act, five decades later, she still was within his thoughts. Only yesterday he looked at a magazine photograph of an old Russian Jewish woman being evicted from her home at the

age of well over a hundred.
His own grandmother was shot
and killed at close range by a
political thug. For speaking
out for Freedom. Dragged out
of the room and shot in the
corridor.

The world was a vile place.
Evil monsters terrorised the
good people. And the
authorities, those who talked
piously, were the worst. The
employers of the state chose
the wickedest employees. The
good were bashed and murdered.

Bloom ran home through the
still blazing town, ran like a
squealing pig and cried out all
his tears until none were left.

That was his grandmother.
His other favourite, Uncle
Lajos, he disappeared still
during the war. The one
contact he had with the adult
world was gone.

Rounded up, he and the other
brothers were allowed home for
Grandfather's eightieth birth-
day. The large dining table
had to be extended, just for
once the whole family was
there.

A photograph fixes the
scene. But they, the
participants, have all
vanished. Uncle Lajos was such
a good person. He bought him a
good pen and a notebook. He

enthused him to become a
writer. People who loved him
for no reason at all. Uncle
Lajos was also murdered but
Bloom was never told the
circumstances. He dared not to
become obsessive. They could
not kill the Grandmother or the
Uncle he knew and remembered.
They were unkillable. But such
bad luck to lose the ones you
love most and have most reason
to love them.

## VII

Not all of it was misery.
There was much laughter, warm
summer nights by the lake. The
year of fun and puns. But on
the whole it was all hop, skip
and jump. No sooner was a
situation established than it
was dissolved. The kiss and
the memory of the kiss and
memory of the same. Airy
nothings. Until the emotional
luggage was full. By now he
was living in rooms stacked to
the top with the trapped souls
of his life. Some boxes have
not been opened for years.

The box containing laughter was
the only one which remained
empty.


# VIII


In desperation qualified by
amnesia, not only his space
contracted but his time ran out
in his efforts to keep all of
his memory alive — so that the
memory of the people should
remain alive in his mind.

But he was no longer a young
person. He had lived for over
30 million minutes by his
unticking watch.

His life encounters on the basis of his having met one person per hour on the average, then he must have met a conservative estimate of 500,000 persons throughout his busy life. Good thing he was not a bee, or a blade of grass.

How did he remember all that immediately available to him which was there only when he thought of it.

All those people, things and circumstances .....

Grandmother alive and well, having travelled from his home town to a holiday resort. Was he four or five years old?

With other children in a
lakeside wooded paradise, the
joy of being a child, the
running, the exhilaration, the
sweet dreams, the little songs,
everything new, fresh, the long
summer, the crisp funny winter,
the slush of spring and golden
leaves of autumn. Running he
fell, a thorn embedded in his
kneecap festered and had to be
cut open to cleanse the wound
adequately. He was a brave
boy. The surgeon did the
operation in a large, sunny
room with French windows to the
garden. He remembered the
faces of the children pressed
against the windowpanes,

wishing him well. Then his beautiful Grandmother arrived from the distant capital, travelled the long journey alone to visit the young invalid. She had brought him an orange and pressed it into his hand. It was warm to the touch and very soft and very sweet. He liked being watched by those gentle eyes. They were still in his mind's eye, unforgotten, sixty years later.

# IX

There they were all in his unpacked suitcase, all those unforgotten people from his First Period, when his language was uncertain and his tasks, definitions, responsibilities, associations, social duties and ties changed inexorably.

Autodidacts are made in this way. The problem was that lack of universal education gave him little indication as to whether his ideas were right or wrong, new or old, significant or insignificant.

*Social duties and ties altered imperceptibly but at an alarming rate. It is not a question of whether truth was involved, the point was that all social obligations changed daily. What he was doing today had a different context from what he did yesterday. Certain things remained very similar but changed nevertheless, not just his bodily looks, but his language, diet, art, work and a network of arbitrary people within which he existed. Stuffed into his suitcase.*

*To describe the first seventeen years of his life as the First Period is, of course,* a brave simplification. The changes in his social status were an amazing if not frightening obstacle race, just like in Voltaire's _Candide_. He was still unwilling to look back on that period with total attention. He wanted to analyse his life in detail, but was unwilling to devote enough time to the task.

The gist of it was that looking back to the First Period he remembered some lovely people coping with impossible situations. One moment he was part of a large family, the next moment they have all been yanked away. One moment it was peace, next moment it was war. What was consistent was his subjection to others, that everything he ever did derived from vague instructions others had given him. No concept was ever his own. In all respects he was not his own man. But barring that vexious thought he had his share of cakes and ale.

# X

For the first six years of
his life he had no idea who he
was. He did not suspect
anything. There were people
around him, lots of arms and
legs and bosoms, very kind and
fussing. His favourite,
recurring dream was going on a
voyage inside a duck-ship's
stomach. The people, while he
was awake toddling about, were
either very big or occasionally
as small as he was and they
lived in a very small world of
a few rooms. The big people
made efforts to be as small as

he was or enfolded him in small bits of their body. He remembered them not just by their looks but also by their touch. His mother's breast which he sucked and a soft arm around his back. All that was pleasantly curious to remember but the voices irritated him. He was now a writer in a different language, and the voices came to him in his childhood's tongue, and he disliked this cruel, see-saw of languages. It was like running from post to post - an impossible task to listen to both languages at once. The thoughts may have been similar *but they changed in translation*

*and with it the truth of the*

*mood in whichever language.*

*The sounds of his childhood;*

*such as;*

"Jancsi, Jancsi, adok neked egy
ötletet", mondta az anyám.

*"Johnny, Johnny, I'll give you*

*an idea", said my mother.*

Ez sokkal későbben lehetett,
talán nem is mondta.

*This happened much later,*

*perhaps she never said it.*

Talán én csak ezt most probálom
kitalálmi.

*Perhaps I'm trying to invent*

*this now.*

Hogy valami értelmet kaphassak
az édes anyámtól.

*So that I can make some sense*

*out of my dear dead mother,*

Mintha az anyám mondaná.

*As if she were still talking,*

Mert valahogy tudom, hogy így
beszélne, ezt mondaná, mert így
beszélt, így gondolkozott és
nekem mindent oda-adott.

*Because in some sense I know*

*that she would talk like this,*

*she would say so, because this*

*was how she spoke, how she*

*thought and she gave me*

*everything she had,*

Az összes gondolatai nyítva
voltak a számomra.

*All her thoughts were open to*

*me,*

Mi tehát lehetett volna az anyám
szavai?

*So what would have been her
words?*

Jancsi, adok egy ötletet, írjál
Nagynénédnek egy levelet
angolúl.

*John, I'll give you a tip,
write to your aunt a letter in
English.*

Mutasd neki hogy már jól tudod a
másik nyelvedet.

*Show her that you are well-
versed in your other language.*

A levél meg lett írva.

*The letter was written.*

Akkor már és még firdogáltam
magyarúl. Nagyon szerettem kis
krokikat írni, már verseket is
komponáltam, nagy bolondos-
ságokat írtam és egészen
megkapott az ihletetség
gondolmánya.

In that time I was still
scribbling in Hungarian, I was
quite fond of writing mood-
pieces, by then I was also
composing poems, also wrote a
lot of nonsense and I was fully
taken by the concept of
inspiration (the world of
thoughts).

Az anyám ötlete megváltoztatta
az életemet.

Mother's suggestion altered my
existence,

Megirtam a levelet angolúl, de
az ihletet is valahogy
megpróbáltam átcsúsztatni,
hínvén azt hogy azt át lehet
tenni az új nyelvbe.

He wrote the letter in English,

but he also tried to smuggle

across somehow the inspiration,

believing that it was

possible to transpose it into

the new language.

Ez egy nagy hiba volt.

This was a tremendous mistake.

Az ihlet dacogni kezdett. Ez
egy új szervezeti élet volt.

The inspiration began to

stammer. This was a different

new network.

Ebben másféleképen kellett élni.
Nem nagyon kellemes.

Here a different mode of life
had to be pursued. Not very
pleasant.


## XI


He was in Newcastle,
visiting his aunt's Geordie
family, (or future family for
then his Aunt and Uncle were
not yet married), in the early
years of his Second Period.

His once and future uncle
took him to see a football
match, the local derby, the man
was a determined Sunderland

supporter. The bus ride he remembered, especially the view and the bridges about the Tyne, and beautiful massive chunky steel structures.

When he commented on this, a sightseer on a bus, the uncle whispered to him from the corner of his mouth, "Stop talking. Everybody can hear you are a foreigner." He thrust his arm out; "That's the town hall." Then in a sideways contorted mouth whisper; "Don't answer. Keep quiet."

Here was then a new set of circumstances. He was obliged to constrain himself to its dictates. He fully accepted the constraints because there was a connecting link which authorised this in the person of his aunt, his father's sister, thus establishing a legitimate succession. If a stranger talked to him like that, he would have to move to another seat. But this man, this uncle, had a right to talk to him like that.

## X I I

Now he did not believe in God. He was interested in every aspect of life and was both very proud and fond of himself. He was going to live to the last moment of his allotted time and when his own death will approach he hoped to hold his head high and laugh. In those days he was given religions, just like new shoes as he outgrown or outworn the ones previous.

He even found young pleasures in living in the ghetto, a newly thrown together ghetto, established at rifle point, by enforced evictions.

He pushed the barrow of his own and his mother's belongings to their new home. His mother was cheerful: what if we lost the silver, the bric-a-brac, we are alive and the sun is shining. Bless her - she was so understanding of the young, pimply boy with the suddenly croaking voice and unwelcome hairs growing in the most unexpected places.

Yes, to be near her in the sireny town, the hot shrapnels whizzing past you, even in the midst of all that cruelty, suffering, of being herded, even that mattered little.


XIII


Then the day of liberation — we have survived. Mother thought of another idea. She calligraphed a beautiful poster. Come for a communal bath, all of you. I want to see you all, naked and unashamed. I shall wash your body clean and tend to your sores. For all that dirt of hatred and of cruelty we must now wash from our bodies and forget forever.

What a communal bath that was. Proud people grew out of the ruins of the still burning town. And whoever was bathed by mother that gloriously cold day of January 1945 has ever since remained clean and pure forever.

The End.